A Garland Series

Classics of Children's Literature 1621-1932

A collection of 117 titles
reprinted in photo-facsimile
in 73 volumes

Selected and arranged by
Alison Lurie
and
Justin G. Schiller

The Gigantick History of the Two Famous Giants and Other Curiosities in Guildhall, London

(two volumes in one)

*with a preface
for the Garland edition by*

Michael H. Platt

Garland Publishing, Inc.

New York & London
1977

Bibliographical note:

This facsimile has been
made from copies in
the possession of
Julian I. Edison.

Library of Congress Cataloging in Publication Data

Boreman, Thomas, 18th cent.
  The gigantick history of the two famous giants
and other curiosities in Guildhall, London.

  (Classics of children's literature, 1621-1932)
  Reprint of the author's 2 volume work: 3d corr.
ed. of v. 1 and 2d ed. of v. 2, originally published
separately with imprint: London, printed for
T. Boreman, 1741.
  Bibliography: p.
  SUMMARY: Miniature guidebooks to the sights of
eighteenth-century London, interspersed with brief
poems and stories.
  1. London--Literary collections. [1. London--
Literary collections] I. Title. II. Series.
PZ7.B64842Gi 1977   823'.5   75-32140
ISBN 0-8240-2256-4

Printed in the United States of America

Preface

It is generally thought that John Newbery
was the first publisher to specialize in books
for children, and as such his name was
borrowed by the American Library Associa-
tion for their annual children's literary
award. Certainly, Newbery was the most
successful and among the most prolific of
eighteenth-century booksellers catering to
the juvenile market—but his efforts were
antedated by those of Thomas Boreman,
equally as innovative a publisher but far less
of a businessman.

Boreman maintained a "stall" in the open
marketplace of Guildhall, "near the two
giants," and from 1740 to 1743 he wrote and
published a series of ten miniature volumes
commonly known as "Gigantick Histories."
These were not Boreman's first writings for
children. Prior to this he wrote the earliest
juvenile work on natural history: *A
Description of Three Hundred Animals; viz.*

Beasts, Birds, Fishes, Serpents, and Insects (London 1730). This work proved quite popular and went through over forty editions by the end of the last century. From its success he developed two supplementary treatises for children: *Description of a Great Variety of Animals and Vegetables* (London 1736) and *Description of Some Curious and Uncommon Creatures* (London 1739), but neither met with mass approval and only the first supplement was reprinted.

Writing children's books for children was a new concept in 1740; the tone of earlier volumes was more pedagogic or moralizing, and the books were seldom illustrated except to display the punishments of sinning in a variety of martyrologies (Janeway, Keach, Bunyan). Thomas Boreman interjected a revolutionary approach into the nursery library; not only would his books be small, so his young readers could hold them comfortably in their hands, but they would also contain pretty woodcuts and be printed from a readable and clear type. His volumes measured less than 2½ inches high and were printed in very limited quantity during the next four years, but they all seemed to be well-received by the public, and several of the titles were even reprinted during this same period. The subject of each of these ten books was some famous London landmark, a descriptive tour written in a rather light style with interpolated verses: the *Gigantick History of the two famous Giants in Guildhall*; *Curiosities in the Tower of London*; *History of the famous Cathedral of St. Paul's*; *A Description of Westminster Abbey*; and a biography of Cajanus, the Swedish giant—actually the story of a person born in Finland in 1709 and filled with anecdotes of foreign travel ending with his present residence in London in 1742.

But besides providing an entertaining text, good woodcut illustrations, and an innovative dwarfed format, Boreman included in each book a list of his juvenile subscribers. While such subscription lists had become usual in works of literature and science, Thomas Boreman was the first to employ this practice in books for children. What a thrill for a youngster to find his name in print in his own reading-book, and how proudly he must have exhibited it to all the household and even more proudly to his playmates—which, in turn, would probably fill them with envy and have them plague their own parents for sufficient money to subscribe for copies next time. Each book was well-bound in a decorative blind-stamped paper over boards and was so entirely appealing that it must be regretted so few copies of these delightful miniatures have survived.

What became of Boreman after 1743 no one knows. Henry R. Plomer records in his *Dictionary of Printers and Booksellers in England 1726-1775* that Boreman occupied three addresses: (1) on Ludgate Hill, near the Gate; (2) The Cock on Ludgate Hill; and (3) Guildhall, 1733-1745(?). At times he was in partnership with Richard Ware, who published the *Description of Three Hundred Animals*, but little else is recorded. He disappeared just at the time John Newbery established his bookshop (1744) at the Bible and Sun, St. Paul's Churchyard. One might like to imagine that Thomas Boreman aided Newbery in his early ventures, but this has never been substantiated; however, he

PREFACE

certainly influenced the type of books Newbery was to publish and made a significant contribution to the history of children's literature.

Michael H. Platt, B.D.S.

MICHAEL H. PLATT has been collecting rare books and first editions since 1964 and spends most of his spare time in restoring and repairing fragile bindings on old children's books. He lives in London with his wife and two children, all of whom share his interest in collecting historical juvenile literature.

THOMAS BOREMAN (fl. 1730-1743)

Bibliography of His Books for Children:
by Justin G. Schiller

*Description of Three Hundred Animals;
Viz. Beasts, Birds, Fishes, Serpents, and
Insects. With a particular account of the
Whale-Fishery. Extracted out of the Best
Authors, and adapted to the Use of all
Capacities; especially to allure Children to
read.* London 1730.

*A Description of a Great Variety of Ani-
mals and Vegetables; Viz. Beasts, Birds,
Fishes, Insects, Plants, Fruits, and Flowers. Extracted from the most consider-
able Writers of Natural History; and
Adapted to the Use of all Capacities, especially for the Entertainment of Youth.*
London 1736.

*A Description of Some Curious and Uncom-
mon Creatures, omitted in the Description of Three Hundred Animals, and*

*likewise in the Supplement to that Book;
designed as an Addition to those two
Treatises, for the Entertainment of young
People.* London 1739.

*The Gigantick History of the Two Famous
Giants, and other Curiosities in Guildhall.*
London 1740. (Second edition, 1740;
"third edition, corrected," 1741.)

*The Gigantick History, Volume the Second:
which completes the History of Guildhall,
London. With other curious matters.*
London 1740. (Second edition, 1741.)

Curiosities in the Tower of London. Volume
I. London 1741. (Second edition, 1741.)

Curiosities in the Tower of London. Volume
II. London 1741. (Second edition, 1741.)

*The History and Description of the famous
Cathedral of St. Paul's.* London 1741.

*The History of St. Paul's. Volume the
Second. To which is added, an Account of
the Monument of the Fire of London.*
London 1741.

THOMAS BOREMAN

Westminster Abbey. Volume I. London 1742.

Westminster Abbey. Volume II. London 1742.

Westminster Abbey. Volume III. London 1743.

The History of Cajanus the Swedish Giant, from his Birth to the Present Time. London 1742.

Selected References:

Stone, Wilbur Macey. *The Gigantick Histories of Thomas Boreman*. Portland, Maine, 1933.

Muir, Percy H. *English Children's Books 1600 to 1900*. London 1954 (reprinted 1969).

Lisney, Arthur A. *A Bibliography of British Lepidoptera, 1608-1799*. London 1960. (See pp. 86-113 for a study of Boreman's natural history titles for children.)

GUILDHALL GIANTS.

THE

Gigantick History

Of the two famous

GIANTS,

And other

CURIOSITIES

In *Guildhall*, London.

Third Edition, corrected.

Printed for *Tho. Boreman*,
Bookseller, near the two
giants in *Guildhall*, *London*. 1741. [Price 4 *d*.

_~~~~~~~~~~~~~~_

During the Infant-Age,
ever busy and always
inquiring, there is no
fixing the attention of
the mind, but by amusing it.

_~~~~~~~~~~~~~~_

DEDICATION.

To all the little masters
    And all the little
        misses
Who are in London town,
And to all the little masters
And all the little misses
In the Country up and
    down;   {more.
And to many hundred
From three years old un-
    to threescore,

This little book I suit,
Which tells of Gogmagog
And of king Brute,
And of his friend Cori-
  neus, who
In sight that mighty giant
  slew.
It tells of many wonders
  more,
Which hastily I've blun-
  der'd o'er,
The like were never told
  before.

The

The PREFACE.

MY little Readers, it would be great pity to send this gigantick Volume into the world without a Preface, when we consider the vast importance of it to all the little boys and girls.

And the chief use we shall make of the Preface, is to inform all the little

A 4   masters

[viii]

masters and misses, that if
they will each of them buy
one of these books,

    Then, very soon
      I'll print another,
    Which, for size,
      will be its brother.
    Such pretty things
      it will contain,
    You'll read it o'er
      and o'er again.

SUB-

SUBSCRIBERS

To this WORK.

A.

MASTER *Jemmy An-*
drews.
Master *Tommy Abney.*
Master *Tommy Allen.*
Miss *Fanny Allen.*
Miss *Polly Andrews.*

B.

Master *Tommy Bowen.*
Master *Maurice Bowen.*
Master *Neddy Boreman.*

[x]

Master *Tommy Boreman*.
Miss *Betsy Bowen*.
Miss *Patty Boreman*.
Miss *Sally Baker*.
Blowze, a Black.

C.

Giant *Corineus*, 100 Books
Master *Oliver Cromwell*.
Master *Tommy Clements*.
Master *Dicky Coleman*.
Master *Jacky Cam*.
Master *Percival Crayker*,
    of Kent.
Miss *Letitia Cromwell*.
Miss *Betsy Clements* 3 Books

D.

Master *Billy Duke*, 7 Books
Master *Joe Duke*, 7 Books.
Master *Jacky Duncombe.*
Miss *Clara Duncombe.*

E.

Miss *Betsy Egerton*, 7 Books.
Miss *Becky Edwards* 3 Books

F.

Master *Matthew Fuller*, 7 B.
Master *Tommy Fullagar.*
Miss *Nancy Fitzer.*
Miss *Polly Fitzer.*

G.

Giant *Gogmagog* 100 Books

L.

Master *Henry Sebastian Leche.*

M.

Master *Jacky Moore.*
Miss *Patty Morrice*, 7 Books

N.

Master *Neddy Newberry.*

O.

Master *Harry Ormes*, 7 Bo.
Master *Billy Oliver*, 7 Bo.

P.

Master *Jacky Watts Parker*, 3 Books.
Master *Benny Procter.*

R.

Master *Jacky Rowe.*
Master *Hedworth Reed.*
Miss *Betty Richardson.*
Miss *Nanny Richardson.*
Miss *Molly Richardson.*
Miss *Sally Redknap.*

S.

Master *Tommy Salway,* 7 Bo.
Master *Tommy Singleton* 3 B.
Master *Tommy Smith.*
Miss *Betsy Singleton,* 3 Bo.
Miss *Nancy Saunders.*
Miss *Patty Saunders.*
Miss *Betsy Sewel.*

[xv]

Miss *Polly Smith.*

T.

Master *Billy Turner.*
Master *Charles Taylor,* and
Master *Grove Taylor,* both
　of Oxfordshire.
Miss *Kitty Thorogood.*
Miss *Elizabeth Taylor,* and
Miss *Anne Taylor,* both of
　Oxfordshire.

W.

Master *Joe Woodgate,* 7 Bo.
Master *Jacky Woodgate.*
Master *Harry Woodgate.*

Master *Neddy Walmesly*.
Master *Neddy Woodcock*.
Master *Elbro' Woodcock*.
Master *Bobby Walling*.
Miss *Nancy Woodgate*, of
    Bartholomew-Close.
Miss *Nancy Woodgate*, of
    Tunbridge.
Miss *Lucretia Wells*.
Miss *Betsy Wilson*.
Miss *Sally Wilson*.

Y.

Master *Billy Yerbury*, 7 Bo.

THE

THE
Gigantick History.

BOOK I.
CHAP. I. *A description of giant Gogmagog.*

AS soon as you enter the great door of Guildhall, look up, right before you, there you will

B   *see*

see those huge giants, one standing on each side of the balcony, about twenty six feet from the floor of the hall, their heads reaching near forty feet.

The old giant we shall call Gogmagog, the young one Corineus, for reasons which we shall tell by and by.

Gogmagog is in height fourteen feet, round his body twelve feet, the length

length of his arm seven,
and of his leg and thigh
five feet: the calf of his
leg is forty two inches in
compass, and his wrist
twenty four inches: his
middle finger is sixteen
inches long, and his great
toe twelve.

His nose is twelve inches
long; his eyes of the size
of tea saucers, and his
mouth, when he opens it,
big enough to take in a

half-

half-peck loaf; and so in
proportion for the rest of
his parts.

In his right hand he
holds a staff seventeen feet
long, with a grabling ball
at the end of it; being
such an instrument of war
as is used by the pioneers,
when they march at the
head of the artillery company, &c. to drive the
enemy out of their tren-
ches, &c.

At

At his left side he has
a sword six feet six inches
long, and at his back a
bow and quiver of arrows.

His habit is like the
ancient Britons, who went
with their bodies great
part naked; only painted
with divers figures to seem
terrible, as they thought,
and thereby make them-
selves more formidable to
the people against whom
they defign'd to make war.

His hair is long, like that of the Druids (a fort of priefts) of old; that of his beard has a fnakie hue, appearing like a number of that vermin interwoven with each other.

He was a giant ftrong and valiant in his time, therefore his head is crown'd with laurel; and he was of a fierce temper, but at the fame time cunning and full of fubtilty.

CHAP.

CHAP. II.

A description of giant
Corineus.

THis giant appears much
younger than Gog-
magog, but of the same
stature, only in the com-
pass of his body and limbs
much lesser, being every
way made more propor-
tionable.

His dress is like that of
B 4   an

an ancient Roman war-
rior, and his body fenced
with exceeding strong ar-
mour, as are likewise his
legs, arms, and wrists.

In his right hand he
holds a halbert of a gi-
gantick size, instead of
the battle-ax, with which
Corineus was wont to
fight, and to do great
execution; and in his left
hand the black spread ea-
gle painted on a shield,
being

being the arms of the
German empire; which
denotes him of that ex-
traction.

The hair of this giant's
head and beard is black
and short; upon his head
he has a strong helmet, or
cap, like that of an ancient
Roman soldier, and upon
his cap a crown of laurel.

He was a hail, robust,
strong, bold warrior; of

a

a lively spirit; but, by reason of his great strength, fierce, proud and haughty.

CHAP.

Chap. III.

*Of the two ancient giants
that were in Guildhall.*

IT is very proper to in-
form my little readers,
that before the present
giants inhabited Guild-
hall, there were two gi-
ants made only of wicker-
work and pasteboard, put
together with great art
and ingenuity: and those
two

two terrible, original giants, had the honour yearly to grace my Lord May-
or's fhew, being carried
in great triumph in the
time of the pageants; and
when that eminent an-
nual fervice was over, re-
mounted their old fta-
tions in Guildhall, which
their fucceffors the pre-
fent giants poffefs, till by
reafon of their very great
age, old time, with the
help

help of a number of City
rats and mice, had eaten
up all their entrails; so
that being no longer able
to support themselves, they
gave up the ghost and
died.

CHAP. IV.

*Of the present giants, their
birth, parentage, and ad-
vancement in the world.*

THE dissolution of the
two old, weak, and
feeble giants, gave birth
to the two present substan-
tial, and majestick giants;
who by order, and at the
city charge, were form'd
and fashioned out of the
trunks

trunks of two gigantick trees, which grew in a certain forest, the name of which I must tell another time. Captain Richard Saunders, an eminent carver in King-street, Cheapside, was their father; who after he had compleatly finish'd, cloath'd, and armed these his two sons, they were immediately advanced to those lofty stations in Guildhall, which they
have

have peaceably enjoyed ever since the year 1708.

But during the thirty-odd years they have been in these high posts, their valet de chambres have often cleaned, new dress'd, and sometimes shaved them; which last necessary article they stand in great need of at this present time, being obliged, by the unreasonable length of their beards, to eat as much hair as victuals. CHAP.

CHAP. V.

A vindication of the giants
reputation and good be-
haviour.

THE two ancient gi-
ants, the grand fathers
of the present, having been
reclaimed from their sa-
vage and brutal way of
living, became so far civi-
lized, that they were de-
servedly promoted to those

C   high

high places in Guildhall,
which they continued in
for many years, time out
of mind, even to the day
of their deaths.

And when those two
worthy old giants had
ended their days, these
their two grandsons, being
the only surviving heirs
that were left of the whole
giant race, laid claim to
their grandfathers inheritance, which the city soon
put

put them in possession of,
and which they have re-
main'd in for upwards of
thirty years, during which
time they have enjoyed an
uninterrupted tranquility,
behaving peaceably to all
mankind ; nor do they e-
ver quit their stations, but
are always constant and
watchful in that great
trust committed to their
care.

Indeed, 'tis said, that

when

when the giants hear the clock at noon strike twelve, they strait step down from off the shelve they stand upon, to eat their dinners, and when they hear the clock at one, they step from whence they come. Tho' this may seem very strange, yet 'tis well known that several gaping fellows have come to Guildhall on purpose to see 'em walk down to dinner; but

were

were always difappointed,
for either they happen'd
to come on a faft-day, or
the giants growing older,
are more fhy of company,
and will fooner go with-
out their meat, than be
ftar'd and yawn'd at all
the while they are eating
it.

C 3   CHAP.

CHAP. VI.

How a certain mighty, rash, bold Caledonian, who destroy'd king Lud and his two sons, conspired against the lives of these two giants; and how the treason was found out by the author of this book; and how the Caledonian will be serv'd, if the giants catch him.

YOU

YOU have heard, my little masters, what credit and reputation these two famous giants always had in this great city; we might therefore have expected, that they would have been suffer'd to descend into their graves in peace, as did their great forefathers of old.

But contrary to all this, a bold Caledonian, or one of Scotish race, who not

C 4 having

having the fear of the
majesty of these giants before his eyes, but being
moved by the instigation
and subtlety of Satan, and
with malice aforethought,
did, with a certain pen
made of a goose-quill, not
worth one farthing, which
he the said Caledonian
held in his right hand,
indite, make, and publish
a certain libel, or tiny
book, call'd the *History of
London,*

London, in which he did most traiterously compass and imagine the total overthrow of these inoffensive and peaceable giants, endeavouring to persuade the whole city to rise in arms against them, between whom there has ever subsisted a good understanding and harmony.

The author of this *Gigantick History*, searching, in expectation of finding
in

in that book great enco-
miums, in praise of the
worthy Guildhall giants,
as indeed who would have
suspected the contrary,
had the good fortune to
discover this deep - laid
plot; and knowing them
to be quiet, good-natur'd
fellows, which he has
prov'd, by being their
next neighbour for above
five hundred days, and for
whom he has a very great
estceem,

efteem, thinks it his duty
to inform the giants of
this black defign againft
them : And makes no
doubt, when they come
to hear it, of being well
rewarded for this honeft
fervice ; and refpected by
his brother citizens, and
all the little mafters and
miffes , for preventing
the deftruction of the giants.

The treafonable words
are

are to this effect : ' That
' the giants in Guildhall
' are scandalous and mon-
' strous wooden statues ;
' that they reflect ignomi-
' ny and reproach on the
' city :' and then, like a
blood - thirsty hardened
sinner, glories that it was
he! procur'd the destruc-
tion of good king Lud,
and his two innocent sons,
off Ludgate ; and that *he !*
in like manner, would ad-
vise

vife the citizens to murder
thefe noble giants.

Don't you think, my
little boys and girls, that
be fancies himfelf as big
as the king's champion on
a coronation day, who
challenges to cut off the
head of him who dares
to contradict what he de-
clares ?

Who can tell ? fhould
he carry his point in this
weighty affair, but that
the

the next thing will be to
advise some body to de-
stroy the lion and unicorn
a fighting for the crown?

And what do you think
is the reason he is so angry
with these giants? Why,
because they frighten fo-
reigners; the French and
Spaniards can't bear the
sight of them, therefore,
he thinks, they ought in
justice to be demolished,
and no longer be suffer'd
(says

(fays he) to continue ob-
noxious to those people !

Sure ! this is treason
   of as deep a dye,
As e'er was hatch'd
    'gainst giant majesty.
And should they it
   once come to know,
They'd chop his head off
   at one blow ;
And, in their
   gigantick wrath,
          They'll

They'll boil his bones
  to make them broth ;
His flesh into
  Scotch-collops cut,
And crack his skull
  like a hazel nut.

CHAP.

Chap. VII.

Why the giants are by some people called Gog *and* Magog, *and by others* Jupiter *and* Mars.

THere are several opinions, which subsist amongst the sage citizens, concerning who these two very famous and huge giants represent.

And I do assure my

D   rea-

readers, it hath coſt me no
ſmall pains to ſearch after
their pedigree amongſt the
monuments of antiquity,
hoping to have found a
clear and diſtinct account
of their lineal deſcent from
the firſt giants, either before, or ſoon after the
flood ; but, to my great
concern, find them all very obſcure in this grand
point.

However, being unwil-
ling

ling to lead my little readers into an error, in fo
weighty an affair, I will
oblige them with a fhort
account of the different
notions which the world
have of thefe two giants,
and fubmit them to their
judgments to determine
which is moft agreeable
to truth.

First then, the moft
common opinion that pre-
vails amongft mankind, is,

D 2   that

that one is Gog and the
other Magog ; but I could
never yet meet with one
perſon that could tell
which was one, and which
the other, or why they
were ſo call'd ; ſo that cal-
ling them by thoſe names
ſeems to have no other
foundation, than that as
the names of Gog and
Magog are mention'd in
ſcripture, which deſcribes
them to be two terrible
monſters,

monſters, ſo they ſuppoſe
theſe to be their repreſen-
tatives.

The next opinion is,
that the old giant repre-
ſents Jupiter, and the
young one Mars; becauſe
the ſpiked ball at the end
of the ſtaff, which the former holds in his hand, they
ſay, is a thunderbolt; and
that the habiliments of
war, which the latter has

about

about him, are the enſigns
of Mars, the god of war.

CHAP. VIII.

*Why the old giant is by
ſome called* Brutus, *and
the young one* Corineus.

THis opinion, that the
old giant repreſents
Brutus, the other Cori-
neus his companion, who
ſlew the giant Gogmagog,
is

is founded upon the following history.

Brutus, they say, after his leaving Troy, meeting with Corineus, a man of mighty fame, and joining company with him and the rest of their Trojan followers; being guided, as he thought, by divine conduct : the oracle of Diana having promis'd, That to the race of Brute, kings of this island, the

whole

whole earth should be subject. Thus encourag'd,
he bends his course to-
wards the west; and, after
some encounters in his
passage, arriving at Tot-
ness in Devonshire, quickly perceives this country
to be the promised end of
his labours.

The island was not yet
called Britain, but Albion,
from a giant nam'd Albion,
the son of Neptune, who
rul'd

rul'd it forty four years,
and gave name to it, after
having subdued the Samo-
theans under the reign of
Bardus: these people were
descended from Samothes,
one of the sons of Japhet,
who, it is said, liv'd about
two hundred years after
the flood. At this time
the island was in a manner
desart, and inhospitable;
kept only by a remnant of
giants, whose excessive
force

force and tyranny had de-
stroy'd the rest of the inhabitants.

Them Brutus over-
comes, and divides the
island among his people,
which he thenceforth calls
Britain. To Corineus,
Cornwall, as we now call
it, fell by lot; or rather
by him chose, because the
hugest giants were said to
lurk in rocks and caves in
those parts; he delighting
to

to exercise his strength on such.

Some time after this, Brutus builds *Troia Nova,* or New Troy, chang'd in time to *Trinovantum,* now London, and began to make laws: and having govern'd the whole island twenty four years, he dy'd, and was buried in his New Troy, (London :) therefore, 'tis said, the citizens, in after ages, erected statues

tues in honour to these
two famous men: to
Brutus, as the founder of
their city; and to Cori-
neus, for destroying all
the giants that infested the
island.

CHAP.

CHAP. IX.

Why the old giant repre-
sents Gogmagog, and how
he happen'd to fall into
the hands of his enemies,
and was kill'd by the
young giant Corineus.

THE last opinion that
I shall mention con-
cerning these two big gi-
ants, and which, for my
own part, I am better
pleased

pleased with than any of
the former, is, that the
young giant represents
Corineus the companion
of Brutus; and the old
one, a mighty giant of
Cornwall, the captain and
leader of all the giant race
in those parts, who having
been worsted in battle, fell
into the hands of Brutus
and his company.

It was customary with
Brutus, and his friends
and

and followers, to keep an
annual festival day on that
shore, where he first land-
ed. On one of these so-
lemn occasions, whilst
Brutus and his people
were in great jollity and
mirth, old Gogmagog,
with a number of his bro-
ther giants, broke sudden-
ly in upon them, and be-
gan a much rougher game
than at such a meeting was
expected, making great
slaugh-

flaughter among them.
But at length, Brutus and
his companions being
more numerous, overcame
them, and kill'd them all
except Gogmagog their
leader; who being a giant
of great fame, was pre-
ferv'd alive to try his skill
with Corineus, who was
likewife a man of mighty
ftrength and ftature: and
a moft terrible battle began between thefe two
fierce

fierce champions; they
were both stout and har-
dy, and victory for a while
hung doubtful: at length,

Old giant Gogmagog,
If story tells no fibs,
With a close Cornish hug
Broke Corineus ribs.

Nevertheless, Corineus,
not at all dismay'd at having three of his ribs broke,
but rather enraged even
to madness, ran furiously

E   at

at the old giant, and heaving him up by main force upon his shoulders, carried him to the next high rock, and threw him headlong over into the sea, where he perish'd; which place is ever since called *Langoëmagog*; that is, the giant's leap.

It appears, therefore, from the foregoing account, that the old giant, as I said, represents an
ancient

ancient Briton, call'd Gogmagog; which in some
measure is confirm'd by
his dress, being like that
of the first inhabitants of
this island : tho' perhaps
not born here, but came
originally from the east,
Asia being the cradle of
the human race, and their
original country : and
some think he was de-
scended from Magog,
whom Moses mentions as

the

the second son of Japhet, the son of Noah.

And the young giant is Corineus, whom learned authors say, was the companion of Brutus, and that he slew the giant Gogmagog. His habiliments, as has been mention'd, are like those of a Roman warrior; yet some think he was descended from Askenez the son of Gomer, the grandson of Japhet,

phet, to whom the Germans owe their origin: But these things are so very knotty, and troublesome to account for, that I must leave them to my little readers to reconcile among themselves: and shall only observe, that as they were two brave giants, that nicely valued their honour, and exerted their whole strength and force in defence of their liberty,

E 3 and

and country; so the city
of London, by placing
these their representatives
in their Guildhall, emble-
matically declare, that
they will, like mighty giants, defend the honour of
their country, and liberties
of this their city; which
excels all others, as much
as those huge giants ex-
ceed in stature the com-
mon bulk of mankind.

I had almost forgot to
tell

tell my little masters, that
the first honour which the
two ancient wicker-work
giants (spoken of in chapter III.) were promoted
to in the city, was at
the Restauration of king
Charles II. when with
great pomp and majesty
they graced a triumphal
arch, which was erected
on that happy occasion at
the end of Kingstreet, in
Cheapside.

E 4   In

In telling things of this
nature, I expect they will
be taken, at first fight, only
for imaginary and idle notions, to say no worse of
them : some perhaps will
object against Guildhall
giants ; and others deny
there ever were any giants,
tho' the sacred scriptures
often mention them ; to
convince such, I give the
following account of giant
Og, king of Bashan.

CHAP.

Chap. X.

A description of the mighty giant Og, king of Bashan.

THis gigantick king was the last of the race of the Rephaims, or vast prodigious men; and from the size of his bed, (which was preserved a long time in the city of Rabbal, the capital of the Ammonites) we may guess at his stature:

ture: It was nine cubits
long, and four cubits
broad; that is, fifteen feet
four inches and an half
long, and six feet ten inches broad. But the Jewish
doctors, not content with
such pigmy wonders, have
improv'd the story to their
own liking: for they tell
us, that this bed of nine
cubits could be no more
than his cradle, since himself was six-score cubits
high,

high, when full grown; that he lived before the flood, and that the waters of it, when at the height, reach'd only up to his knees; that however, he thought proper to get a-top on the roof of the ark, where Noah supply'd him with provisions; not out of any love to him, but that the men who came after the deluge, might see how great the power of

God

God was, which had de-
stroy'd such monsters from
the face of the earth. See
Calmet and *Munster*.

THis my FIRST BOOK
    does things contain
Full pleasant to
    the merry train
Of masters smart
    and misses pretty,
Living in or near
    great London city.
CHAP. I. and II.
   we do describe   Two

[61]

Two famous giants
    and their tribe;
'Their arms and equi-
    page are ſhewn,'
And in CHAP. IV.
    their ſire's made known;
There you may alſo
    quickly read,
How the two ſons
    were born and bred.
In CHAPTER III.
    I did relate
The two old giants
    diſmal fate,

                    Who

Who were eaten up
   by city rats :
O blufh for fhame,
   ye London cats !
In Chapter V.
   the giants right
Defended is
   'gainft foes defpite.
Chap. VI. we blow'd
   when piping hot,
The Caledonian's
   horrid plot,
For which his bones
   muft go to pot.
           Chap.

CHAP. VII. and VIII.
   the titles tell
Of th' giants, and where
   they us'd to dwell.
In CHAPTER IX.
   you read the story
How Corineus
   fought for glory ;
By Gogmagog
   his ribs were broke,
But his stout heart's
   like heart of oak.
Brave Corineus !
   the conq'ror, he
           Threw

Threw Gogmagog
　　into the sea.
CHAP. X. contains
　　an odd remark,
Og rides astride
　　on Noah's ark.
The giants now
　　their course have run;
And, for this time,
　　my work is done.
The SECOND BOOK
　　will plainly show
All in Guildhall
　　you want to know.
The End of the first Book.

❀❀!❀❀❀!❀❀!❀❀

BOOK II.

Chap. I.

Of Guildhall, *when it was first built, its bigness,* &c.

Guildhall is the great court of judicature for the city of London, where meetings of the

F   citi-

citizens are held for the election of officers, solemn entertainments, and for transacting all their business relating to the government of that great city.

This stately building was begun in the mayoralty of the right honourable Sir Thomas Knowles, in the year 1411, and was finish'd ten years after.

And in the year 1425,

in

in the mayoralty of John
Coventrie, Efq; the lord
mayor's court was begun
to be built, next the may-
or's chamber, or orphan's
court, and the old council
chamber adjoining, were
added: and laftly, the
ftately ftone porch at the
fouth entrance of the hall
was erected.

Some time after, a
kitchen was added, for the
convenience of holding

their

their publick entertainments in Guildhall; and about the year 1501, Sir John Shaw, then lord mayor, kept the firſt feaſt of mayoralty in the ſaid hall.

This grand fabrick ſuffer'd much in the fire of London, in 1666, but was rebuilt in 1669, being well repair'd and beautified, both inſide and out.

This ſpacious hall is in length

length 153 feet, in breadth 48, and about 55 in height, and will hold seven or eight thousand people.

CHAP. II.

Of the pictures of the Kings, Queens, and Judges; the flags, &c.

AT the east end of the hall, over the court of hustings, are the pic-

F 3   tures

tures of fix kings and queens, all curiously painted at full length, and placed in the following order.

His most gracious majesty, king George II. and his late queen Caroline, are in the middle, one on each side the judge's chair, facing you; on the right hand of king George, is queen Anne; and on her right hand, king

king William : and on the
left hand of queen Caro-
line is king George I. and
on his left hand, queen
Mary, king William's
queen.

Both the sides and weſt
end of the hall, are em-
belliſh'd likewiſe with the
pictures of two lord keep-
ers of the great ſeal, and
twenty judges, all painted
in full proportion, in their
proper robes, and are pla-

F 4   ced

ced in the following or-
der.

On the south side, next
to queen Mary, are

1 Sir Heneage Finch,
   lord keeper.
2 Sir Orlando Bridgman,
   lord keeper.
3 Sir Matthew Hale.
4 Sir Richard Rainsford.
5 Sir John Kelynge.
6 Sir Edward Turner.
7 Sir Samuel Brown.
8 Sir Thomas Tyrril.

9 Sir

9 Sir William Windham.
10 Sir John Archer.
11 Sir William Morton.
   And next to him, over
   the sheriff's court, at
   the west end of the
   hall, are
12 Sir Timothy Littleton.
13 Sir Edward Thurland.
14 Sir William Ellys.
   On the north side, next
   to Sir William Ellys,
   are
15 Sir Hugh Windham.
              16 Sir

16 Sir William Wyld.
17 Sir Christopher Turner.
18 Sir Edward Atkins.
19 Sir Thomas Twisden.
20 Sir Francis North.
21 Sir John Vaughan.
22 Sir Robert Atkins.

The pictures of these great men, were put up by the citizens in their common hall, out of gratitude for their honest service, in determining justly the differences between land-

landlords and tenants,
without expensive law-
suits, when the city of
London was rebuilding,
after the great fire in 1666,
pursuant to an act of par-
liament for that purpose.

Next see those streaming
   flags,
Which up aloft do hang;
Tho' now they look like
   rags,
Shew, we the French did
   bang.

In December, 1706.
queen Anne prefented to
the city twenty fix ftan-
dards, and fixty three colours, to be hung up in
their hall; but there was
room only for forty fix colours and nineteen ftan-
dards.

Thefe were all taken by
the duke of Marlborough,
at the battle of Ramillies
in Flanders, fought on
Whitfunday, 1706, upon

a

a total defeat of the French
and Bavarian forces, who
had ten thousand men kil-
led, and six thousand taken
prisoners; among whom
were above five hundred
officers, many of them of
great note; with all their
tents, baggage, and am-
munition, fifty one pieces
of cannon, several kettle-
drums, and upwards of
one hundred and twenty
standards and colours.

Chap.

Chap. III.

*Of the arms of the twelve
chief companies, &c. the
fiue clock, and the hall-
keeper's office.*

THE walls on the north
and south sides of
Guildhall, are adorn'd
with fourteen pilasters of
the Gothick order, paint-
ed white and veined blue,
their capitals or heads gilt
with

with gold ; and above the
capitals are finely painted
the king's arms, thofe of
the city, and its twelve
chief companies ; namely,
the Mercers, Grocers,
Drapers, Fifhmongers,
Goldfmiths, Skinners,
Merchant-Taylors, Ha-
berdafhers, Salters, Ironmongers, Vintners, and
Clothworkers.

If the Lord Mayor be
of any other company
when

when he is elected, he
muſt be made free of one
of theſe twelve, to qualify
himſelf to ſerve that office.

At the eaſt end of the
hall are the arms of St.
Edward the confeſſor, and
the ſhield and croſs of St.
George. At the weſt end,
the arms of the confeſſor,
thoſe of England, and the
arms of England and
France quarterly.

In the front of the bal-
cony,

cony, between the two giants, is a fine clock; which was put up in the year 1730, when Sir Richard Brocas was lord mayor. Upon the top ſtands old Time with a young child in his arms, which he is beginning to eat: this figures to us, that as time is the parent that produces all things, he no ſooner brings forth his children but he begins to devour

G them.

them. And on each fide
of the clock, there is a
cock in the action of crow-
ing; which reminds us of
watchfulnefs in fpending
our time; with other em-
blematical figures, all cu-
rioufly carv'd.

On each fide of the
ftone fteps going up from
the great hall, are the
Hall-keepers offices; round
the top of each of them
are fix iron palm-trees of
curious

curious workmanſhip, ſer-
ving as props to the large
balcony over head. And
on the outſide, upon the
iron-work of each office,
are fix'd

S. P. Q. L.

in golden letters, which
ſtand for the Latin words,

*Senatus Populuſque
Londinenſis.*

In plain Engliſh, 'tis all one
As, The Senate and Peo-
ple of London.   Cн.

[85]

Chap. IV.

*Of that terrible place
call'd* Little ease.

THese two difmal pri-
sons are fituated under
the Hall-keepers offices,
among rats, mice, and
other vermin ;

With ceilings built
  fo rough and low,
The ftubborn Boy
  is forc'd to bow ;

G 3   And

And to bring him
    ftill the lower,
Down he muſt ſit
    upon the floor;
Becauſe not of
    ſufficient height
For a big Boy
    to ſtand upright.
Theſe priſons are
    to puniſh crimes
Which 'prentice Boys
    commit ſometimes.
The Chamberlain
    does mildly try

                   To

To make the naughty
   Boy comply,
With all the marks
   of tenderneſs
That a fond parent
   wou'd expreſs
To check a diſ-
   obedient ſon,
Who does the paths
   of ruin run :
And what he bids
   is only this,
To pardon beg
   fcr what's amiſs,
      G 4   ·   And

And promise on
  his bended knees
No more his Master
  to displease.
How like is this
  t'indulgent heav'n!
That bids us ask,
  and be forgiv'n?
But if this easy
  task won't do,
To make his stomach
  buckle to,
Then to that dismal
  place he's sent

                   Of

Of sad disgrace
    and punishment;
From whence he can't
    get out again,
Till favour'd by
    the Chamberlain.
If after all
    he'll not repent,
To Bridewel he
    straitway is sent:
What kind of treatment
    he'll find there,
I have not heard,
    nor can declare;

                    But

But bad enough
  I do not doubt;
So take great heed
  that you keep out.

CHAP.

Chap. V.

*Of the court of Huſtings,
court of Conſcience, She-
riff's court, &c.*

AT the eaſt end of the
hall, on a theatre, is
weekly held the ancient
court of Huſtings, being
the ſupreme court of ju-
dicature within the city of
London; as that of the
Common Council is of its
legiſlature.   The

The judges of this court are, the Lord Mayor and Sheriffs for the time being: And when any matters of moment are to be try'd in this court, the Recorder sits with them, to direct them in points of law, and to give judgment.

And occasionally, the Lord Chief Baron of the Exchequer sits here, upon trials of Nisi prius.

And

And before the said
Huftings is held the court
of Requefts, commonly
call'd the court of Confci-
ence; for the recovery of
debts under forty fhillings.
Their court-days are Wed-
nefdays and Saturdays,
from twelve to two.

At the weft end of the
hall are held the Sheriff's
courts, Wednefdays and
Fridays for Woodftreet
compter, and Thurfdays
and

and Saturdays for that of the Poultry. The judges of this court are, Mr. Serjeant Urling, Deputy-Recorder of this city, and John Stracy Esq;

In the corner, on the north side of the Sheriffs court, is the door that leads into the kitchen belonging to Guildhall.

CHAP.

Chap. VI.

Of the Chamberlain's office, the Mayor's court, &c.

AT the head of the steps, on the right hand, is the Chamberlain's office, where he holds his court for making free, enrolling, turning over, and hearing and determining complaints between masters and apprentices.

And

And facing the steps
which lead from the com-
mon hall, is the Mayor's
court, wherein the Com-
mon-Council meet, Ses-
sions of the Peace are held,
causes determin'd before
the Lord Mayor, and his
assistant the Recorder of
the city. And here also
the Lord Chief Justice of
the King's-Bench, sits upon trials of Nisi prius.

On each side the judge's
seat

feat are the chriftian Virtues: firft, Prudence, with
a ferpent in her right
hand, and a looking-glafs
in her left; the looking-
glafs reprefents her caution
in undertaking, the fer-
pent her wifdom in per-
forming what fhe has un-
dertook.

The fecond reprefents
Juftice, with a fword in
her right hand, and a pair
of fcales in her left: the

H   fcales

scales teach us that funda-
mental maxim, both in
reason and religion, of do-
ing as we would be done
unto: and the sword is to
execute vengeance for the
breach of it.

The third is Religion,
with a book seal'd up in
her right hand, and one
open in her left: the seal'd
book signifies Faith, the
open one Practice; which
two make up the sum of
all religion.   The

The fourth is Fortitude, holding part of a pillar on her knee; which shews she is the support of all other virtues.

On the left hand as you enter the Mayor's court, is the court of Orphans: and farther on is the new council chamber; on the left of that, is the old council chamber. And beyond that is a room in which one of the Aldermen daily sits as justice. C H.

CHAP. VII.

Of the new Council-chamber.

THis magnificent room was erected in the mayoralty of Sir Thomas Middleton, in the year 1614; since which time it has been used as the council-chamber, wherein the Lord Mayor and Aldermen hold their court.

Their court-days are

Tues-

Tuesdays; but on some particular occasions they meet on other days. The right honourable the Lord Mayor and twelve Aldermen make a court.

The Ld. Mayor sits facing the great door, his seat being raised above the rest. On his Lordship's right hand sits the Recorder, and the Aldermen who have serv'd the office of Lord Mayor, promiscuously on

either

either hand, excepting the late Lord Mayor, who for a month after he is out of his office, sits next my Lord, on his left hand; during which time he is also address'd by the title of *Lord*; that the grandeur of the highest magistrate may not be laid down at once, but by degrees.

Lower and farther from the chair sit those Aldermen who have not serv'd

Lord

Lord Mayor; as also the two Sheriffs, if Aldermen. The Town-clerk, &c. at the table.

In this beautiful room are six pieces of tapestry; five of which are very curious, and represent the history of Nebuchadnezzar.

The first, on the right hand when you enter the great door, is the worshiping his golden image, *Dan.* chap. iii. ver. 1, &c.

H 4　　The

The second, between the windows, is Shadrach, Meſhach and Abednego, going into the fiery furnace, *Dan.* iii. 19, &c.

The third, in the dark corner next my Lord's chair, is Nebuchadnezzar proclaiming the God of Shadrach, Meſhach, and Abednego, to be the only true God, *Dan.* iii. 29, &c.

The fourth, in the corner on the other ſide of the chair,

chair, is Daniel interpreting the dream of Nebuchadnezzar, *Da*.iv.19,&*c*.

The fifth, which is on this side the last, is Nebuchadnezzar's transformation, *Dan*. iv. 28, &*c*.

The sixth, between the two doors, is the story of Leander swimming cross the Hellespont to Hero.

Over the chimney of the same room, is a curious piece of painting : it was

was prefented to the city by the late Sir James Thornhill; and, 'tis faid, has been valued at above five hundred pounds.

It is painted in chiaro ofcuro, that is, light and fhade; which affects the fight fo as to appear like brafs or metal.

In the middle fits Juftice, with a pair of fcales in her left hand, and in her right the fword of juftice,

OR

on which is the cap of maintenance: she, reaching her hand over the shoulder of Londini, rests the handle of the sword upon her heart.

Londini sits lower, resting on the city arms, crowned with laurel, holding an olive branch in her left hand.

On the left side of Justice is Liberty, with the cap upon the end of a staff.

Close

Close by her is Piety with her cross, and a chalice of incense flaming.

Beneath, is an half figure, representing Truth, holding in her left hand the sun in a circle, and pointing to it with her right.

On the right hand of Justice, in the corner, is an ancient Roman : he holds a spear in one hand, and a shield in the other,

on

on which is a thunderbolt,
fignifying power. And be-
fore him is a Roman ma-
tron ; and at their feet a
little naked boy, holding
an eagle in his arms.

Over the Lord Mayor's
feat are the king's arms,
and over the door, thofe of
the city, finely carv'd :
and round the border of
the cieling the arms of
eighty one Lord Mayors
of London, neatly paint-
ed ;

ed ; the last being those of
Micajah Perry, Esq; Lord
Mayor in the year 1739.

In the oval in the mid-
dle of the cieling, is represented London in the form
of a beautiful matron, sitting upon the clouds,
crown'd with towers: in
her left hand is the city
arms, behind her Pallas,
the goddess of war and
wisdom ; and under her
are two boys, one with the
sword

sword of justice upon his
shoulder, the other pointing to the cap of mainte-
nance, and the mace lying
under her feet. Before her
is Peace, presenting her an
olive branch ; and Plenty
with her horn, pouring out
riches.

In four compartments,
two at each end of the
oval, are the four cardinal
Virtues, represented like
little boys. Those next
the

the door are, Prudence, with his glaſs; and Temperance, with his cup: at the other end, Juſtice with his ſword, and Fortitude, reſting on a pillar.

The borders of theſe compartments, and of the oval, &c. are embelliſh'd with fruits and foliage of exquiſite workmanſhip, richly laid on with gold.

For the reſt, I muſt refer the reader to my 2d Volume.

The E N D.

THE

Gigantick History,

VOLUME the SECOND.

Which completes

The HISTORY of

Guildhall, London.

With other curious

Matters.

The Second Edition.

London, Printed for *Tho.*
Boreman, near the giants
in *Guildhall*, and at the
Boot and Crown on *Lud*
gate-hill. 1741. [Pr. 4 *d.*

SUBSCRIBERS
To the
HIST. of GUILDHALL.

VOL. II.

A.

MASTER *Tommy Allen*.
    Miss *Fanny Allen*.
Miss *Jenny Austin*, 7 Bo.

B.

Master *Warner Barret*, 7 B.
Master *William Augustus*
   Baker.
Miss *Nanny Bransill*, 7 Bo.

A 3   Miss

Miss   *Bradgate*, 8 Books
Miss *Kitty Bull*, of Ongar
   in Essex, 7 Books.
Miss *Nelly Blackbourn*, 4 B
Miss *Betsy Blackbourn*, 4 B.
Miss *Nanny Bayley*.
Miss *Nanny Boehm*.
Miss *Jenny Boehm*.
Miss *Polly Buck*.
Miss *Anna Maria Brewer*.
Miss *Becky Booth*.
Miss *Anna Bridges*.
       C.

Giant *Corineus*, 100 Books
       Master

[vii]

Master *Johnny Clarke*, 14 B

Master *Jarvise Carr*, 7 Bo.

Master *Harry Clark*, 7 Bo.

Master *Natty Causton*, 7 Bo.

Master *Henry Cromwell*, 7 B

Master *Georgy Cork.*

Master *Billy Curtis.*

Master *Anthony Chapman.*

Miss *Nanny Cromwell*, 7 B.

Miss *Sally Cornwell.*

Miss *Polly Corrie.*

Miss *Kitty Carbonell.*

Miss *Betsy Carte.*

Miss *Polly Corbett.*

A 4   Master

[viii]

D.

Master *Jemmy Duke*, 14B.

Master *Jacky Deveil*. *

Master *Tommy Drake*.

Master *Sammy Drake*.

Miss *Polly Du Gard*.

E.

Master *Tommy Emlyn*.

Master *Sollom Emlyn*.

Miss *Becky Edwards*, 7Bo.

F.

Master *Tommy Furly For-*
ſter, 3 Sets.

Master *Benny Forſter*, 3 Sets.

Master

* *Jacn.*

Master *Jacky Fenner*, 3 Bo.

Miss *Betsy Fenner*, 3 Books.

Miss *Jenny Fletcher*, in Cheapside.

Miss *Alice Fenwick*.

Miss *Nanny Fenwick*.

Miss *Sukey Franklin*.

G.

Giant *Gogmagog* 100 Books

Miss *Nanny Louisa Goring*.

Miss *Frances Goring*.

Miss *Sukey Gore*, 14 Books

H.

Miss *Henny Hitchcock*, of Oporto.

[x]

Master *Dicky Holmes*, 7 Bo.
Master *Charles Horne*, 7 Bo.
Master *Jacky Hadley.*
Master *Harry Hadley.*
Master *Tommy Hunt.*
Master *Billy Hucks.*
Miss *Nanny Hucks.*
Miss *Molly Hucks.*
Miss *Herriot Hucks.*
Miss *Sally Hucks.*
Miss *Kitty Hoskins.*
Miss *Cocky Halfhide.*
Miss *Jenny Hutchinson*, of
Bruntwood.
Miss *Polly Hillman.*

O.

Master *Duke Olive*, 3 Books
Master *Billy Oliver*.
Miss *Patty Oliver*.

P.

Master *Benjam. Pyne*, 10 B.
Master *Harry Parker*, 7 Bo.
Master *Alexander Parker*.
Miss *Sally Pryor*, 7 Books.
Miss *Betsy Parish*.

R.

Master *Ralphy Radcliff*, 7 B.
Master *Tommy Rickman*.
Master *Billy Rickman*.
Miss *Penny Radcliff*, 7 B.

Miss *Rebecca Rickman.*
Miss *Polly Readshaw.*

S.

Master *Jacky Scantan* 3 Sets
Master *Billy Spinage,* 3 Bo.
Master *Tommy Smith,* of
    Abingdon.
Master *Joshua Simmons.*
Master *Allyn Simmons.*
Master *Jacky Sedgwick.*
Miss *Betsy Steward,* 7 Bo.
Miss *Polly Smith,* of
    Abingdon.
Miss *Sarah Savile.*
Miss *Nanny Savile.*

Miss *Martha Savile.*
Miss *Mehetabel Simmons.*
Miss *Peggy Scot.*
Miss *Sally Stauley.*

T.

Master *Francis Tradin.*
Master *Joe Hart Turner.*
Miss *Polly Hart Turner.*
Miss *Hannah Totty Tomkins.*
Miss *Fanny Titty Tomkins.*

W.

Master *George Hughes*
  Worsley.
Miss *Polly Worsley,* of
  Hertford.

To all my
Kind SUBSCRIBERS.

I Know you began to think me very tedious in bringing out this SE-COND VOLUME of the *Gigantick History.*

But, perhaps, you did not know, that *Necessity,* the mother of *Invention,*

B   was

was the author of the First
Part; which as soon as
she had finish'd, left me,
and sent *Success* in her
stead : now this last lady
and I had been long stran-
gers, and altho' she has
lived with me about three
months, we know not
how to behave to each
other: In short, she is a
very desirable person, but
much fitter for pleasure
than business: *Necessity*,
for

for invention and diſpatch, is worth two of her; and if the latter had not ſtept back again to begin the work, I fear the former, whoſe task it was, would never have finiſh'd it.

I foreſee, what I have to tell my readers will be of ſuch an intolerable length, that I ought to divide it into chapters.

However, I muſt inform my little maſters and miſ-

[xx]

ſes, that this book, which completes the hiſtory of Guildhall, is not what I promis'd in the firſt wou'd *ſuch pretty things contain,* that's to come hereafter.

But I do aſſure my little readers, what is contained in this, was deſigned to be all in the firſt volume, had not *Contrivance,* one of the daughters of *Neceſ-ſity,* perſuaded me to the contrary.

She

[xxi]

She urged, that such a
huge volume would come
too dear for children, and
be too heavy to carry in
one pocket ; it was therefore better to have two ;
one for each, which would
ballance them so equally,
there would be no fear of
their growing lap-sided,
from the weight of such a
gigantick work.

You'll agree with me,
that these arguments ap-

B 3   peared

peared so reasonable, that
the old lady *Prudence*, who
ought to govern us all,
would have blamed me if
I had not complied with
them. Now,

Of my masters
  and my misses
  I this favour ask,
That they agree
  to encourage me
To do the other task.

I

I mean, each of them
to buy one of these second
parts :

Then I'll run
And quickly finish
what's begun.

But not too fast: I must
remember the old cau-
tion ;

B 4   When

When work's in haſte
    beſure take heed
To work no faſter
    than good ſpeed:
For too much hurry,
    ſweat and toil,
What wou'd be well
    does often ſpoil.

THE

THE
Gigantick History.

BOOK III.

CHAP. I. *Of the four ancient statues on the outside of Guildhall.*

BEFORE you enter Guildhall, you will observe

obſerve under the fine
balcony four ſmall ſtone
ſtatues, two on each ſide
the porch, which are ve-
nerable for their antiquity
and eſcaping the great fire
of London ; and which,
it is likely, were ſet up
when the great porch was
firſt built, about three
hundred and twenty years
ago.

By their dreſs and ha-
bit, they appear to be ladies

dies of great nobility as
well as antiquity, two of
them having coronets on
their heads ; but who they
reprefent, we will not take
upon us too nicely to de-
termine, feeing all our city
hiftorians have left us very
much in the dark in this
particular; but fhall give
the conjectures of our
learned antiquarians and
others concerning thefe
figures, and fubmit them,

as

as heretofore we did a
knotty affair about the giants, and as we shall all
other difficult points, to
my little readers, to settle
amongst themselves.

Some persons are of opi-
nion that these figures represent four eminent ladies
who were at the head of
a conspiracy, said to be
formed by the English
women, for killing all the
Danes which were in the
land,

land, by each cutting the
throat of her bedfellow at
an appointed hour, to re-
venge their injured hus-
bands, whose places the
lordly Danes had insolent-
ly usurped.

I can't tell what credit
my little masters and misses will give to this con-
ceit; but, for my own
part, I believe those images were placed there on
some other account. How-
ever,

ever, we'll pass to the second notion, and when we have heard all, we may perhaps, by each other's assistance, have the good fortune to discover more of this intricate affair.

They have been called the four cardinal virtues, *viz.* Prudence, Temperance, Justice, and Fortitude. But these names, we are told, they received from the artful fancy of a

poet,

poet, who was one of the
attorneys of the sheriff's
court about a hundred
and seventy years ago, the
better to preserve them
from the violence of the
people, who were, in the
times he wrote his verses,
very busy in defacing and
pulling down all images,
as popish saints, and relicks
of idolatry.

So that we find, my
little masters, that there
was

was a brave champion in
those times, who stood up
in defence of these ancient
and curious statues, as well
as in our days there ap-
peared a stout one in de-
fence of the Giants of
Guildhall.

The next conjecture is,
that they represent four
noble ladies, of as many
different nations, who
have been friends to this
city ; namely, a Roman,

a

a Saxon, a Dane and a
Norman ; becaufe, fay
they, their drefs or habits
are different. But as there
appears little or no reafon
to fupport this conjecture,
we'll leave it, and hear the
next.

The fourth is, that the
firft figure on your left
hand, which reprefents the
oldeft perfon, is Maud the
emprefs, who was born in
London ; and the next,

Boadicea, which the shield
she rests her left hand upon, and likewise her long
tresses, in which that great
princess is usually figured,
is thought to confirm:
under her conduct, the
Britons, in the reign of
Nero, conspired to reco-
ver and regain their liberty. The other two sta-
tues are imagin'd to be her
daughters, Venutia and
Camilla.

Others

Others have thought
one to be queen Philippa,
wife to king Edward the
third, who gained great
love of the citizens by reafon of a requeſt ſhe once
made for ſome of them,
on her knees, before the
king and council.

Whoever they reprefent,
we may be ſure, my little
readers, they were good
friends to Liberty, becauſe
they are trampling upon

Tyranny and Barbarity;
the figures of four rough
men lying under their feet,
which old Time has so
nibbled, that two of their
heads are eaten off, and
their other parts so wasted,
that they have almost lost
the human form.

It was the custom in
former times, to set up on
publick buildings the effi-
gies of patrons and bene-
factors; as well in honour
to

to the memory of such de-
serving persons, as for the
imitation of succeeding
generations.

And that these are such
monuments, is all, I think,
that we can resolve with
any certainty from them.

C 3   Chap.

CHAP. II.

Of the other images ; and
of the companies arms, &c.
in the front of Guildhall.

JUST above the balcony
are the figures of Moses
and Aaron ; who represent
law and divinity: and over
the window, near the top,
the king's arms finely car-
ved in stone, and gilt ; and
at a little distance on each
side,

fide, the city fupporters, being two dragons with their wings expanded.

On the right fide of the porch, under the balcony, are the arms of England, and on your left hand thofe of Edward the confeffor; and round the lower part of the balcony, the arms of thirty four of our city companies, painted in their proper colours, and placed in the following order.

C 4   At

At that end next the chapel are, 1. Embroiderers, 2. Innholders, 3. Masons, 4. Painters, and 5th the Carpenters: The first in the front, next to the last mentioned, is the Butchers, 2. the Cutlers, 3. Wax-chandlers, 4. Armourers and Braziers united, 5. Pewterers, 6. Brewers, 7. Clothworkers, 8. Ironmongers, 9. Haberdashers, 10. Skinners, 11. Fish-

Fishmongers, 12. Grocers,
13. Mercers, 14. Drapers,
15. Goldsmiths, 16. Merchant-Taylors, 17. Salters,
18. Vintners, 19. Dyers,
20. Leather-sellers, 21
Barber-Surgeons, 22. Bakers, 23. Tallow-chandlers, and 24. the Girdlers;
and next to that, round the
corner, 1. Sadlers, 2. Cordwainers, 3. Plumbers, 4.
Curriers, and lastly the
Founders.

This

This stately front fortunately escaped the great fire in 1666, tho' the upper part of the hall suffer'd much; the upright walls, which before were only about thirty five feet in height, are now twenty feet higher; and eight large windows added on either side; and the roof, which was formerly built sloping, and met at top, as in Westminster hall, and

com-

common buildings, is now flat, leaded over, and adorned with battlements.

CHAP. III.

Of Guildhall chapel; and of the images on the out-side.

THIS chapel is on the right hand, adjoin-ing to Guildhall: It was
built

built about four hundred
and forty years ago, and
dedicated to St. Mary
Magdalene, and All saints:
the upper part of it was
burnt at the fire of Lon-
don, but most part of the
walls were preserved.

There are three niches
in the front toward Guildhall yard, enriched with
columns, entablature, &c.
of the composit order,
supported by demy-lion,
griffin,

griffin, terms, &c. in
which are the figures of
king Edward the sixth,
queen Elizabeth, and king
Charles the first in armour,
treading upon a globe:
These were all set up of
latter times; 'tis likely,
when the chapel was re-
paired after the fire in
1666.

Over the great window
in the front is a small image
of our Saviour in stone.

And

And over the dial on the upper corner of the chapel, is a large figure of a man kneeling on his left knee, with a ſtar upon his head, which repreſents Heſperus. He turns his face towards the weſt, or ſun ſetting; ſignifying his conſtant attendance on that planet; he ſhining the laſt of all the ſtars in the morning, and appearing the firſt in the evening.

Heſpe-

Hesperus, 'tis said, lived some time in Italy, which from him was called anciently *Hesperia*. He frequently went up to the top of mount Atlas, to view the stars: at last, he went up, and came down no more. This made the people imagine that he was carried up into heaven; whereupon they worshipt him as a god; and called a very bright star after his name,

name, Hesperus; which
is the evening star, and
sets after the sun: but
when it rises before the
sun it is called Phosphorus,
or Lucifer; that is, the
morning star.

This same Hesperus was
father of those three girls,
from him call'd *Hesperides*,

Who gardens had
in which, we're told,
Grew trees that bore
apples of gold. And

And this rich fruit
    was safely kept
By a watchful dragon,
    whilst they slept:
Till Hercules,
    as poets say,
The dragon kill'd,
    and stole the fruit away.

Perhaps, my little mas-
ters, they only gave out
that a dragon watch'd it,
to frighten boys from their
orchard; and these famous

D   apples

apples might be only gol-
den pippins, or, as some
have thought, oranges.

CHAP. IV.

*Of the inside of Guildhall
chapel.*

THIS chapel is small
but neat: It has six
handsome windows on the
north and south sides, and
two large ones in the east
and

[51]

and weſt; the pulpit and desk are plain; and at the weſt end there is a particular ſeat for the Lord Mayor, over which is a gallery; and round the walls are thirteen pieces of tapeſtry; an hiſtorical account of which, will be the ſubject of the following chapters.

There are very ſeldom any ſermons preached in it; but during the time

D 2　　　　　St.

St. Paul's was rebuilding,
the sermons now preached
at that church by appoint-
ment of the bishop of
London, were preach'd in
Guildhall chapel every
Sunday morning: and in
case St. Paul's is shut up
at any time, my Lord
Mayor comes to Guildhall
chapel.

Such of my readers as
desire to see the inside of
this fine chapel, must
come

come of a Tuesday about eleven a clock; at which time, unless it be holiday, the Lord Mayor usually attends divine service, before he goes to hold the court of Aldermen.

D 3　CHAP.

Chap. V.

An explanation of the tapestry in Guildhall chapel.

THE piece behind the communion table, represents Paul and Barnabas at Lystra, mention'd *Acts* the xiv^{th}.

WHILST those apostles were preaching at Lystra, a poor cripple, lame from the hour of his birth, being

ing one of their hearers,
was obſerved by St. Paul,
who ſaid to him, *Stand
upright on thy feet*; and
by the bare ſpeaking of the
word, his feet were made
ſo ſtrong that he leaped
and walked.

When the people ſaw
it, they concluded this
miracle could not be done
but by the immediate pre-
ſence of the Deity ; and
therefore, running about

in great confusion, they
cried out, That the gods
had put on human shape,
and were come down a-
mong them. They looked
on Barnabas as Jupiter, the
supreme god; and Paul,
as Mercury, the interpre-
ter of the will of the gods,
because he spoke more
than Barnabas.

But as soon as this mira-
cle came to the ear of the
priest of Jupiter, he came
to

to Paul and Barnabas, bringing oxen with garlands of flowers on their horns; being such victims as they offered to the gods they worshiped, intending to offer sacrifice to the apostles: But they abhorring such idolatry, rent their garments in detestation of it; endeavouring by arguments drawn from some of the plainest instances of nature, such as

day,

day, night, summer, winter, &c. to convince them, that worship was due only to that God who was the author of all those blessings; yet this discourse, so pressingly urged by the apostles, could scarce restrain those poor idolators from sacrificing to them.

THE pieces spoke of in the seven following chapters, contain the history of Moses, and the deliverance of the Israelites.

Chap. VI.

Moses and the burning Bush,
Exodus iii.

THIS is the first piece
on the left hand in
the chancel.

God pitying the grievous oppressions of the Israelites, appeared to Moses
as he was looking after his
father in law's flock on
mount Horeb, in a bush
all

all on fire, but not con-
sumed. Moses, amazed at
this unusual sight, turned
aside, to see if he could
discover the cause of this
surprizing event. God
knowing his thoughts,
called to him out of the
midst of the bush; bidding
him not presume to ap-
proach too near, but pull
off his shoes, a token of
reverence amongst the eas-
tern people, because the
place

place whereon he stood
was holy ground ; that is,
made holy by the divine
presence.

Chap. VII.

*Moses first appearing before
Pharaoh*, Exod. v.

THIS piece is the next
in the chancel to
that last spoken of.

WHEN Moses was call'd
to

to go upon this sacred errand, so great was his modesty, that he would fain have excused himself from that weighty office, tho' called to it by the Almighty. However, being encouraged by God, and accompanied by his brother Aaron, he went in and told Pharaoh, *Thus saith the Lord God of Israel, Let my people go, that they may hold a feast unto me in the*
wil-

wilderness. Pharaoh replied, That he neither knew the Lord, nor would he let Ifrael go : and thereupon ufed them more cruelly.

C H A P. VIII.

The making of the bitter waters fweet, Exod. xv.

THis piece is alfo on your right hand in the chancel.   THE

THE Israelites having cross'd the Red sea, arriv'd at the wilderness of Shur; where they march'd three whole days, and were extremely faint for want of water. The next place of their encamping was Marah; where was water enough, but so bitter that they could not drink it; which occasion'd a general murmuring among them. But Moses, by the divine

direc-

direction, found a tree, which when he had cast into the waters, they became sweet.

There the people were admonished to continue firm and constant in their obedience to God, and then they should not suffer those plagues and diseases which he had brought on Egypt.

E   CHAP.

Chap. IX.

The gathering of Manna,
Exod. xvi.

THIS is the fourth
piece in the chancel.
THE children of Iſrael
in their journeyings came
to the wilderneſs of Sin ;
where they murmured a-
gainſt Moſes and Aaron,
and expreſſed their wiſhes
that they had continued
in

in Egypt, where they had no want of any thing, rather than come into this defart, to perifh with hunger.

God, who heard their murmurings, to let them fee that he was able to fuccour them in their greateft extremities, fent them that evening fuch a quantity of quails, or feathered fowls, as covered the camp ; and in the

E 2   morn-

morning, large quantities
of a small round substance,
like the hoar-frost, which,
after the dew was exhaled,
they perceiv'd, and called
manna. It was so solid
that it would bear grind-
ing in a mill, or pounding
in a mortar ; and yet easi-
ly melted by the heat of
the sun.

This, Moses told them,
was the bread that God
had given from heaven :
and

and he ordered them to
gather every day for a
man an omer, which is ra-
ther more than two quarts
of our measure : but on
the sixth day they were to
gather two omers a man ;
one of which was to be
referved for the day fol-
lowing, which was ap-
pointed to be a Sabbath,
or day of reft, fanctified
to the Lord. This man-
na ferved the Ifraelites for

E 3   bread

bread about forty years,
till they came to the con-
fines of the land of Ca-
naan. *Exod.* xvi.

Chap. X.

*Moses's rod turned into a
serpent,* Exod. vii.

THIS is the fifth piece
of tapestry in the cha-
pel, facing the pulpit.

AARON, by the com-
mand

mand of Mofes, caft down
his rod before Pharaoh and
his fervants, and it was
fuddenly changed into a
ferpent. Pharaoh imme-
diately fent for the magicians of Egypt, the prin-
cipal of whom feem to be
Jannes and Jambres, men-
tioned by St. Paul; who
cafting down every man
his rod, changed them
likewife into ferpents; or
fo impos'd on the fenfes of

E 4   the

the spectators, by giving
them an appearance of life
and motion, that they
could not discern them
from real and living ser-
pents; or perhaps, by help
of some of the spirits of
darkness, so swiftly remov-
ed the rods, and placed real
serpents in their room, that
the standers by could not
detect the fallacy. How-
ever that was, Aaron's serpent swallowed up theirs.

Pha-

Pharaoh, according to the divine prediction, remaining obdurate, and perhaps the more so for seeing what the magicians had done, and refusing to hearken to Moses and Aaron; God order'd Moses to take the rod, which had been a serpent, and charge Aaron to lift it up over the river Nile, and other waters of Egypt, and they should become blood.

CHAP.

CHAP. XI.

Moses striking the rock,
Exod. xvii.

THIS piece is next to
that spoke of in the
last chapter.

WHEN the children of
Israel came to Rephidim,
near mount Horeb, the
people murmuring again
for want of water, Moses,
as he had received orders
from

from God, ftruck with his rod the rock in Horeb; from whence iffu'd ftreams of water in great abundance.

___

C H A P. XII.

The deftruction of Pharaoh and all his hoft in the Red fea, Exod. xiv.

THIS piece is on the left hand fide of the Lord Mayor's feat. THE

THE king of Egypt had no sooner suffered the departure of the children of Israel, but he began to repent; and reckoning them shut up, and, in a manner, imprisoned in the wilderness, pursued after them with six hundred chariots, and a great number of horse and foot.

The Israelites, who were encamped by the Red sea, seeing such an army in pursuit

pursuit of them, murmur-
ed against Moses, and were
ready to wish that they
had been content with
their Egyptian slavery.
Moses bade them lay aside
their fears, be still, and
they should see the salva-
tion of the Lord to them:
that God himself would
fight for them against their
enemies: and that those
Egyptians, of whom they
were so much afraid,
should

should be seen of them no
more after this day.

Then the Lord order'd
Moses to bid the people
go forward ; and lift up
his rod over the sea to
divide it. And the pillar
of the cloud was between
the camp of the Egyp-
tians and that of the If-
raelites ; being a cloud
and darkness to the for-
mer, but giving light by
night to the latter; so that
the

the one came not near the
other all night long.

Moſes, having received
his orders, ſtretch'd forth
his hand over the ſea; and
the Lord by a ſtrong eaſt-
wind cauſed the ſea to go
back all that night; and
ſo divided the waters, that
the people might paſs over
on foot upon dry ground.
So the Iſraelites croſſed
the Red ſea without the
leaſt difficulty.

The

The Egyptians observing this division of the waters, which had made the passage easy to the Israelites, resolved to take the opportunity that seemed to be put into their hands, of pursuing them the same way with the utmost speed. Some time after they had been in the sea, God caused their chariot wheels to fall off; and bade Moses stretch forth

his

his hand over the sea, that
the waters might return.
Which being done ac-
cordingly, the waters re-
turned with that prodigi-
ous force, that, all hope
of succour being lost, Pharaoh, his chariots, horses,
and their riders, and all
his army soon perished
in the sea. Many carcases
were seen by the Israelites
floating on the waters, and
many driven by the vio-

F   lence

lence of the stream to the opposite shore.

Upon this occasion Moses composed a song of praise and thanksgiving, in very sublime strains of poesy, which he and the people sang; and his sister Miriam the prophetess, with a great company of women, with timbrels and dances.

The remaining five pieces are the history of king Saul. CHAP.

CHAP. XIII.

Saul's meeting the maids going to draw water, 1 Sam. ix.

THIS, which is the first piece of tapestry relating to Saul, is on the right hand side of my Lord Mayor's seat.

WHILST the Israelites persisted impatiently in their desire of a king, it

hap-

happened, that Kish a
Benjamite, one who made
a confiderable figure in
his tribe, having loft his
affes, fent his fon Saul,
who was a well-favoured
perfon and very tall in
ftature, with a fervant to
feek them. So, after they
had travelled thro' many
places in vain, and Saul
feemed willing to return
home, perfuaded by his
fervant, he went to inquire
after

after Samuel: *And as they went up the hill to the city, they found young maidens going to draw water;* who told Saul where he should find the seer, meaning Samuel: and according to their directions, they found him going to the high place, where a sacrifice was to be offered; and Samuel acquainted him that the asses were found.

F 3　CHAP.

Chap. XIV.

Samuel's entertainment of Saul, 1 Sam. ix.

THIS is the second piece on the north side of the chapel.

SAMUEL, having informed Saul that the asses were found, intimated, that the affections of the people were faſtned on him and his family. Saul modeſt-

modeſtly expreſſed his un-
worthineſs of ſuch eſteem,
from the ſmallneſs of his
tribe, and the meanneſs of
his family in it. After
which, Samuel took him
and his ſervant, very hoſ-
pitably entertained them,
and ſet them in the chief-
eſt place among thoſe that
were invited, who were
in number about thirty.

F 4   CHAP.

Chap. XV.

Samuel's anointing Saul,
1 Sam. x.

THIS piece is next
the pulpit.

Some time after Samu-
el's entertainment of Saul,
when they were got into
the city, they privately
discoursed together, the
servant being ordered to
pass on at some distance;
Samuel

Samuel took a vial of oil and poured it on Saul's head; saluted him, and let him know, that the Lord had appointed him to be captain over his inheritance: And that after his departure he should meet two men, who wou'd certify him that the asses were found, and of the concern his father was in for his absence.

CHAP.

CHAP. XVI.

Saul's meeting the three men with three kids, and three loaves, and a bottle of wine, 1 Sam. x.

THIS piece is plac'd next to Samuel's entertainment of Saul, spoken of in the fourteenth chapter.

SAMUEL, after he had acquainted Saul that the asses were found, further
told

told him, that from thence going to the plain of Tabor, he should meet three men going to Bethel, one carrying three kids, another three loaves of bread, and another a bottle of wine. That they should salute him, and give him two loaves of bread, which he should receive of them. Saul departing from Samuel, found all those signs verified that day.

CHAP.

CHAP. XVII.

*Saul and his armour-bearer
killing themselves,* 1
Sam. xxxi.

THIS is the laſt piece of
tapeſtry, and is plac'd
next but one to the pulpit.

THERE having been a
very ſharp battle ſought
between the Iſraelites and
the Philiſtines, in which
the whole army of the
former

former was routed; the three sons of Saul, Jonathan, Abinadab, and Malchishua were slain: and Saul himself was so sorely wounded with the arrows of his enemies, that in despair he bade his armour-bearer kill him: which he refusing, he fell upon his own sword; but, according to Josephus, not thrusting it home enough, and espying a certain Amalekite,

lekite, he defired him to
flay him, which he accord-
ingly did; and pofted a-
way to carry tidings of
it to David.

Saul's armour-bearer
feeing his mafter dead,
immediately fell upon his
fword, as he had done,
and died. When the If-
raelites, who were on the
other fide of the valley,
and on the other fide of
Jordan, perceived that
                    their

their army was routed,
and the king and his fons
were slain, they quitted
their cities, and the Phi-
liftines came and inhabited
them.

HAVING now told
my readers all the curiofi-
ties, that I know of, both
within and without-fide of
Guildhall; and likewife of
the chapel adjoining: I
     fhall

shall next entertain them
with an account of my
Lord Mayor's Show;
which I believe will be
agreeable to my little
masters,

    Because by this
       they all may see
    What in good time
       they'll come to be.

The End of the third Book.

❀❀!❀❀❀!❀❀!❀❀

BOOK IV.

An account of
My Lord Mayor's
SHOW.

CHAP. I.

*Of my Lord entring upon
his office.*

MY Lord Mayor is
the grand magif-
trate

trate of this great city. He
is yearly elected on Mi-
chaelmas day, and though
the oldest Alderman, who
has not served that office,
is usually chosen, yet that
is at the electors discretion.

On St. Simon and Jude's
day, the 28th of October,
let it happen to be Sun-
day or any other day ; the
Lord Mayor, Aldermen,
Sheriffs, &c. meet at
Guildhall about twelve

a clock : and when the
Lord Mayor elect comes,
they all go to the Hustings
court ; where, after the
common crier has com-
manded silence, the Town-
clerk gives the new Lord
his oath, and then the old
Lord Mayor rises up, and
gives the new his place :
The Chamberlain first
presents the sceptre to
him, then the keys of the
common seal, and lastly,

the seal of the office of
mayoralty; and the sword-
bearer brings him the
sword; all which the
Mayor immediately re-
turns. This ceremony be-
ing ended, they ride home
in their coaches to dinner;
the Aldermen who have
been Mayors accompany-
ing the old Lord Mayor,
and those who have not
served that office go with
the new Lord. The next
morn-

morning, the 29th of Oc-
tober, called *Lord Mayor's
Day*, they meet together
again, and proceed as
follows.

CHAP. II.

*Of my Lord Mayor's pro-
cession to the water side.*

THE Lord Mayor elect
meets as many of his
brethren the Aldermen as
G 3   pleas

please to come, at Guild-
hall, about eleven a clock
in the morning; all be-
ing invited: where hav-
ing breakfasted, about 12
they set out in the following order.

BEFORE the procession
go officers to clear the
way: Then the first in
the cavalcade are the
streamers of the company
the new Lord is free of,
born by sturdy watermen:
next

next come the band of
pensioners, as many in
number, they say, as my
Lord is years old, headed
by their captain : and after them the gentle-
men ushers, called *rich
batchelors*, thirty in number, with white staves in
their hands, and chains of
gold about their necks, all
in black clothes. Then
comes the musick, *viz.*
kettle-drums , trumpets ,

haut-

hautboys, and other muſi-
cal inſtruments; next the
three banners; the King's
in the middle, the City's
on the right hand, and the
Lord Mayor's on the left.
Then comes the maſter of
the city barge in his
gown; and after him the
champion, or maſter of
defence, with his drawn
ſword in his hand; next
to him march thirty or
forty whifflers, dreſs'd up
                    with

with ribbands, and white staves in their hands; who are followed by the two beadles of the old Lord's company; and then come the master, wardens, and livery-men in their gowns. After them follow the new Lord's company in order, with all their attendants. And before the coach come first the sheriff's officers, then the city musick, the city marshals on horse-

horseback, finely capara-
son'd; the city artificers,
in furr'd gowns; and next
before the coach, my
Lord's officers.

And so they proceed
to the end of King-street,
Cheapside, where the old
Lord Mayor's coach falls
in next that of the new
Lord. The swordbearer
is at the right side in the
new Lord's coach, with
the sword in his right
hand,

hand, and cap of mainte-
nance upon his head ; and
on the left fide of the
coach, the common crier,
bearing the mace.

After the old Lord's
coach, come the Alder-
men paft the chair, in their
coaches, according to fe-
niority : next the Recor-
der, and after him the Aldermen who have not
ferv'd Mayor : Then come
the Sheriffs, Chamberlain,
Town-

Town-clerk, Comptroller, city Remembrancer, Common Hunt, city Solicitor, and city Counsel.

Being thus marshalled, they proceed with the greatest uniformity to the water side; and at the Three Cranes stairs they embark on board their state barge.

CHAP.

Chap. III.

Of the procession by wa-
ter, &c.

THE barge being well
provided with all things
fitting for the voyage, the
cockfwain takes the helm,
and the bargemen their
oars, and fo fet forward
towards Weftminfter; at-
tended by a great number
of the city companies in
their

their barges, all with en-
signs, streamers, &c. dif-
play'd ; mufick playing,
and thoufands of boats
crowded with people, to
fee this gallant fhow ; being all the way faluted
with a difcharge of the
great cannon from the
wharfs, and batteries on
both fides the river, with a
' God fend the fhip a good.
' voyage, and blefs the.
' Lord Mayor, and his ho-
                    ' nour-

' nourable company.' And, if wind and tide are not too boisterous, in about one hour they reach Westminster stairs; where they are receiv'd by a large body of city grenadiers, who fire a volley to welcome their landing.

Then they walk to Westminster hall, where the new Lord Mayor is shewn the several courts; and having paid his respects

spects to the Judges, &c.
then sitting, he is sworn,
according to custom, be-
fore the Barons of the Exchequer. Then they go
round the hall again, and
invite the Lord Chancel-
lor and Judges of the several courts to his Lordship's
feast. This being ended,
they return back to their
barge; and are again sa-
luted in their passage with
a discharge from the great
guns;

guns; and attended by several companies in their barges, with their streamers, banners, musick, &c. as in coming. And about three or four a clock my Lord lands, generally at Blackfriars stairs; where another large body of the honourable artillery company receive him and his attendants, and give them three vollies.

H   CHAP.

CHAP. IV.

*Of the proceſſion to Guild-
hall.*

FROM Blackfriars ſtairs
they commonly pro-
ceed up the Ditch-ſide in
their coaches to Ludgate
hill; where the Nobility,
Judges, &c. who are in-
vited to dine with my
Lord, join the proceſſion:
the artillery company, his
Lord-

Lordſhip's company, &c.
marching before. And
thus this ſolemn, magni-
ficent, and grand procef-
ſion, is conducted with
great regularity thro' the
city to Guildhall, amidſt
thouſands of men, women,
and children, who fill the
balconies and windows,
and line both ſides of the
ſtreets, from the landing-
place, all up the Ditch-
ſide, Ludgate hill and

H 2 ſtreet,

ſtreet, St. Paul's church-
yard, Cheapſide and King-
ſtreet, to Guildhall.

When his Lordſhip
comes near the hall, the
commanding officers of
the artillery company line
both ſides of the way, till
my Lord, the Nobility,
Judges, and all the great
perſonages who attend this
grand ſhow, enter the hall.

CHAP.

CHAP. V.

Of my Lord Mayor's feaſt.

MY Lord and his honourable gueſts having enter'd the hall, aſcend the theatre built over the Huſtings, at the eaſt end; and ſeating themſelves in order at a table, where the cloath, napkins, &c. are made up and placed with great art and beauty; they

H 3   are

are presently entertained
with a most sumptuous and
elegant feast.

The Lady Mayoress,
the Aldermens Ladies, and
others of quality, dine on
the Hustings, with my
Lord. And at the west end
of the hall is another table
for more of that sex.

In the body of the hall,
the Swordbearer has a ta-
ble for himself, and the
officers belonging to my
Lord.   There

There are besides three
or four guest tables, for the
gentry invited.

The hall, on this occa-
sion, is illuminated with a
great number of lights, and
suitable decorations added.

Under the feet of giant
Corineus, is built a gallery
for the musick, who play
whilst my Lord and the
company are at dinner.

After dinner, there is
fine dancing, and other

H 4   decent.

decent mirth, till 'tis time to retire to their respective homes.

Many of our Kings and Queens have honour'd the Lord Mayor's feast with their presence: and it is particularly recorded of Sir Henry Picard, Lord Mayor in the year 1356, that he feasted at his table at one time, the kings of England, France, Cyprus, and Scotland.

CHAP.

Chap. VI.

Of the city Companies that grace my Lord's show.

I Should have told my readers, that when my Lord lands at Blackfriars, all the Companies that attended him in their barges, land likewise; and with streamers, musick, &c. in great pomp, grace this majestick show. Some **Companies** have stands built

built along the sides of the streets through which my Lord passes; where they seat themselves in order, and pay their respects to his Lordship, the Aldermen, &c. as they come by.

And those Companies who have not barges, meet at their halls, or usual places, and either walk in procession, or otherways demonstrate their joy on this festival day. And when

when my Lord and his
honourable friends have
got safe to Guildhall, or
where his feast is kept, all
the city Companies, in
their livery gowns, pro-
ceed gravely to their re-
spective halls, &c. where
they all have elegant and
plentiful dinners provid-
ed, and good liquor of all
sorts in abundance.

But I must not forget
to inform my little masters
of the following hero. Cu.

CHAP. VII.

Of the Man in Armour.

THIS champion bold
    in bright aray,
Looks like St. George
who did the dragon flay.

He is clothed with ar-
mour of polifhed fteel,
which covers his whole
body, legs, arms, fingers
and toes, made with fuch
partitions, fo as to bend
                    any

any part of his body, excepting his feet; which, for want of proper joints, if by any accident he should be unhorsed, he would be unable to remount himself: and upon his head he wears a strong helmet.

This armour he has from the Tower : It weighs about a hundred and a half; which the horse he rides on chiefly sustains.   This

This heavy armour was made use of by valiant knights in former times, who voluntarily offered to vindicate in single combat their country's honour.

About twelve a clock this mighty champion, mounted on his horse, with a great drawn sword in his hand, advances at the head of the worshipful company of armourers, who

who set out from their
hall in Coleman-street,
and proceed to a large
house near Trig stairs,
belonging to that com-
pany; where having re-
galed themselves, they set
out again; going through
St. Paul's church-yard,
Ludgate, and so on to
Salisbury court in Fleet-
street; where having just
show'd themselves, they
return back, and march
before

before my Lord's com-
pany through the city to
King-ftreet, and then to
their own hall in Cole-
man-ftreet : and after this
bold champion hath feen
the worfhipful company
fafe hous'd, he difmounts
his prancer; and fo con-
cludes the ceremony.

The E N D.